SNOOPING CAN BE

Regrettable

Books by Linda Hudson Hoagland
from Jan-Carol Publishing, Inc:

LINDSAY HARRIS MURDER MYSTERY SERIES:
SNOOPING CAN BE DANGEROUS
SNOOPING CAN BE CONTAGIOUS
SNOOPING CAN BE DEVIOUS
SNOOPING CAN BE DOGGONE DEADLY
SNOOPING CAN BE HELPFUL–SOMETIMES
SNOOPING CAN BE UNCOMFORTABLE
SNOOPING CAN BE SCARY
SNOOPING CAN BE REGRETTABLE

THE BEST DARN SECRET
ONWARD & UPWARD
MISSING SAMMY

SNOOPING CAN BE

Regrettable

LINDA HUDSON HOAGLAND

Jan-Carol
Publishing, Inc

"every story needs a book"

Snooping Can Be Regrettable
Linda Hudson Hoagland

Published August 2020
Little Creek Books
Imprint of Jan-Carol Publishing, Inc.
All rights reserved
Copyright © 2020 by Linda Hudson Hoagland

ISBN: 978-1-950895-54-0
Library of Congress Control Number: 2020944228

You may contact the publisher:
Jan-Carol Publishing, Inc.
PO Box 701
Johnson City, TN 37605
publisher@jancarolpublishing.com
jancarolpublishing.com

This Book Is Dedicated To My Sons:
Michael E. Hudson
Matthew A. Hudson

DEAR READER

Lindsay Harris, mother of Emily, Ellen, and Ryan, has to face the most unanticipated event in her life when her youngest child, Ryan, is involved with drug dealers. He is only 11 years old and she is at a total loss on what she should do to get him out of this mess.

Lindsay's dream of a tame, normal life has evaporated and she along with her friend, Jed, must do the job for the police when they are attacked in her home.

Lindsay is no different from any other single mother, except that she is determined that her children should survive all of the evils the world has to offer.

How to stop the evils of the drug world from taking over Ryan's life and the lives of the remainder of her family becomes her focus.

This story tells you, the reader, what Lindsay had to do to help her son, and she learns along the way that snooping can be regrettable.

ACKNOWLEDGMENTS

Janie C. Jessee, publisher of eleven of my books, must be acknowledged for allowing me to do what I must do—write.

A special thanks to Tammy Robinson Smith for asking me to start this little series.

Chapter 1

"Ryan, where have you been?" I asked my tardy eleven-year-old son.

"I was with Devon," he said sheepishly.

"Why are you so late?" I demanded.

"We just lost track of time. My watch stopped ticking and my cell phone battery died, or I would have called you when I found out I was going to be late. Honest, Mom, I would have called you."

"Go on and get your dinner that I saved for you in the microwave. Don't be doing this again. Do you understand me, Ryan? Don't do this again. Don't do this again," I repeated, so the thought would stick in his mind.

I watched him walk away into the kitchen, and wondered about the strange look in his eyes.

It's just your imagination, Linds. He's just an eleven-year-old boy, I thought.

I was trying to convince myself that there was absolutely nothing strange about the look on Ryan's face and deep within his eyes. I brushed off the bad thoughts and went on about my business of picking up after three active kids.

My identical twins, fourteen-year-old daughters Emily and Ellen, kept telling me to pay attention to Ryan's friends. I tried to do that, but the names he mentioned as friends changed daily—except Devon. Devon was always hanging around Ryan.

I asked my girls what they meant by "pay attention to Ryan's friends," but their only answer was a shrug. If they weren't going to tell me anything, then I didn't know what I should be looking for. After all, he was only eleven. What could he get into with his friends? Of course, that was a question that I would regret not having answered.

I didn't have it in my mind that things had changed so much since my own youthful days. It never occurred to me that the adult problems could trickle down to kids as young as Ryan. I could understand the temptations affecting my teenage daughters, but the thought of an eleven-year-old boy dealing with adult issues was hard to accept.

I cornered Ellen and Emily and tried to get them to tell me what was happening.

"You girls are around your brother more than I am," I said sadly. "I have to work to support us with food and clothing. That sort of keeps me away a lot more than I would like. Please tell me what is going on in Ryan's life that I don't know about."

"It's drugs, Mom," said Emily. "He has been hanging around some boys who are selling and doing drugs."

"What?! What kind of drugs? He is only eleven years old. Where is he getting them? What is he taking?" I sputtered angrily.

"He gets them from his buddies at school," said Ellen.

"Who? What buddies? I thought I knew all of his friends. They all come from fine, upstanding families," I said skeptically.

"You don't know all of his friends. Fine and upstanding families doesn't mean they can't do or sell drugs," said Emily.

"Why didn't you girls tell me this was happening?" I demanded.

"We did tell you. Actually, we told you to check out his friends. Don't you remember?" asked Ellen.

"Yes, I did check out his friends—or at least those he told me about at that time. Have they changed?"

"Some are new, but those 'fine, upstanding' boys are the ones to watch," said Emily, the cynic of the twins.

"Look it up on the internet, Mom. I'm sure there's something on there that can help you figure out what to do next," said Ellen.

"Ellen, Emily, *you* aren't doing anything like that, are you?" I asked.

"Of course not, Mom. We've seen what the drugs have done to some of our friends, so we've stayed away from the dealers and the drugs," said Emily.

Ellen nodded her head in agreement, and I was grateful for that much.

I did check the internet, and was directed to rehabilitation centers of all kinds.

I read horror stories of all kinds about youngsters addicted to drugs. Some of them would kill to get their next fix or pill.

Is Ryan that far into drugs? If so, why didn't I know about it? Do I have to go that route for an eleven-year-old boy?

Chapter 2

I gave Ryan some time to eat, then I told him I needed to talk with him. He didn't look too happy about the talk, but he walked to his bedroom with me right behind him.

He had started sit, or fall, onto his bed when I grabbed him.

"Look at me, Ryan."

"Why?!" he snapped.

"Just look at me. *Now*," I said sternly.

He glanced up and down and around the room. He obviously didn't want me to see his eyes.

"*Now*, Ryan! *Look at me now*," I said, with anger creeping into my voice.

He brought his downcast eyes up to look into mine.

"What are you looking for?" he asked softly.

"I found it," I answered.

"Found what?" he asked in a shaky voice.

"I found my reason for this little talk," I said sadly.

"What are you talking about, *Mom*?" he asked me with a bit of sarcastic emphasis on *mom*.

"Don't use that tone with me ever again, Ryan. Do you understand me?" I said sternly.

"Yes, ma'am."

"I am talking about the condition of your eyes. Did you know that certain drugs you swallow or smoke affect your eyes? Of course you do. That's why you didn't want to look at me."

Ryan didn't say anything. He fidgeted, inspecting his fingernails and kicking at the bedspread corner that was hanging to the floor near his foot.

"What have you taken, Ryan? For that matter, how did you take it?" I demanded.

"Nothing! I didn't take nothing."

"Your eyes tell me you did. What was it?" I demanded.

"I swear, Mom, I didn't take anything."

"Then why do your eyes look that way?" I asked.

"I was standing in the same room with someone who was smoking marijuana. That's all, Mom. I didn't take nothing and I didn't smoke nothing."

"Who was doing the smoking?"

"Just a friend."

"What friend? Tell me a name, Ryan. I want to know a name right now," I said harshly.

"I can't, Mom. I don't want him to get into trouble," said Ryan in a pleading tone.

"You mean trouble like you are in? Isn't that right?"

"Yes, I guess so."

"The name, Ryan, I want the name."

"I can't. I promised I wouldn't tell anyone," he whispered, like the eleven-year-old child that he was.

"You know you will be punished, don't you?" I said solemnly.

"Yeah, I guess."

"What do you think your punishment should be?" I asked.

"I don't know. What are you going to do to me?"

"I need to think about it for a while. I'm too upset with you to do anything right now. I'm going to sleep on it until I decide," I said angrily. "In the meantime, you are grounded. You are to come directly home as soon as you get out of school, and go straight to your room to do your homework."

"How long am I grounded?" he asked.

"I don't know yet."

Leaving the room, all I wanted to do was cry. He was my baby. I didn't want my baby involved with any kind of drug. I didn't want him to know any drug dealers.

How did that happen? For that matter, why didn't I see it happen to my Ryan?

Chapter 3

I went to bed with the feeling of absolute failure.

How could I not notice that my son was hanging out with druggies? Why didn't I pay more attention to what was happening around me? Why couldn't I have been a better mother?

I could rationalize and answer all of those questions, but I wasn't happy with the answers I came come up with.

My life wasn't easy. I had a job and many, many responsibilities that filled my head and my time. None of those responsibilities were more important than those of taking care of my children, however.

I tossed and turned most of the night as I tried to figure out my next step.

Ryan was not a drug addict—not yet. I wanted to make sure that he didn't become one before he even got out of the seventh grade.

Grounding him and not allowing him to hang around with his friends after school might help, but what about during school hours? Those kids were in the same classes as Ryan, so he would see them every day.

I didn't want to go to the teachers and tell them that Ryan and his buddies were doing drugs. What if they weren't? What if it was someone else who was smoking pot around Ryan?

I could be falsely accusing them of something that they might not be part of. How could I find out? Ryan was not going to be a snitch.

Finally, the questions faded and my mind slowed down enough to go to sleep for a short time. The alarm blared too soon, pulling me out of the sleep I wanted to continue for a bit longer.

I forced my body from the bed and went about my morning duties to get myself going so I could go to work. But first, I had to rouse my three sleeping beauties: Ellen, Emily, and Ryan. They had to get up and get ready for school, and that was always a chore—each and every morning.

I knocked on Ellen's bedroom door until I heard a response. Next I went to Emily's door, and I had to knock a little harder to get her attention.

Across the hall from Emily was Ryan's bedroom, where I would usually knock and wait for a response, then knock again, and sometimes pound on his door a third time before he was actually awake enough to get dressed. Ryan was always difficult to rouse from sleep. Most of the time he would answer and roll over to go back to sleep.

The girls were busy getting dressed and listening to their music choices for the morning, but there was still no sign of Ryan stirring.

His dragging around and waiting to the last minute to get dressed would cause him to miss the school bus. I certainly didn't want that to happen, because then I would have to drive him to school; that would make me late for work, which would anger Wayne, my boss.

"Let's go, Ryan!" I shouted through the closed bedroom door. "You need to answer me now. So let's go."

No response.

I turned the doorknob and discovered that the door would

not open. There was something blocking me from entering his room.

"Ryan Harris! Open this door right now!" I shouted angrily.

Again, no response.

Ellen and Emily popped their heads out of their bedrooms to find out about the commotion I was causing in the hallway.

"Mom, is everything all right?" asked Emily.

"I can't get Ryan up for school, and I can't get into his bedroom. Both of you girls come here and help me open this door," I shouted.

Emily pushed on the door and yelled, "Ryan, open the door right now!"

I had no idea what was up against the door. They didn't have locks on their bedroom doors. I did have one on mine, but I was the mom in this family.

"Ellen, go outside, walk around to Ryan's bedroom window, and see if you can look through it. He might have already opened the blinds."

"Okay, Mom, but we've got to hurry or we'll miss the school bus," replied Ellen.

"Don't worry about the bus. I'll take you to school if you miss it," I said, trying to hide my irritation with Ryan.

Emily continued to push on the door and yell at Ryan.

"Stop the yelling, Em. He isn't going to answer. But we do have to get in there and see what is going on," I said angrily.

Ellen came busting back into the house saying, "I can't see inside, but the window isn't closed completely. I need something to climb up on so I can get inside."

"Get the stepladder out of the back room. I'll come with you and help you get inside. Em, you keep pushing on the bedroom door. We'll get inside, one way or another," I said slowly through clenched teeth.

I followed Ellen to Ryan's window and held the ladder in

place while she climbed up to push it open.

"Do you see anything, Ellen?"

"Give me a second," Ellen replied. She struggled to push the window up far enough to climb inside.

"Well?" I asked impatiently.

"Ryan's on the bed, and his chest of drawers is against the door."

"What? Let me see," I said. Ellen crawled down the ladder.

I climbed up the ladder and forced myself through the open window.

"Ryan? Ryan, wake up," I said, crossing the room to his bed.

He started moving a bit, so I knew he wasn't dead. That thought had raced through my mind when I initially saw him lying there.

I moved to the chest of drawers and pulled it away from the door.

"You can come in now, Emily," I said loudly.

"Ellen, take the stepladder back inside and then come to Ryan's room," I shouted.

Ryan was beginning to rouse himself back to reality.

"What is wrong with you, Ryan?" I asked. I tried to brush his hair back out of his face; I wanted to see his eyes.

"Nothing. I was asleep, that's all," he said through a haze that I knew still filled his mind.

"Why did you move your chest of drawers against the door?" I demanded.

"What?"

"You heard me."

"Heard what?"

"Stop it, Ryan Harris. Why did you move the chest?" I snapped.

"I didn't want anyone to come in uninvited," he slurred.

"Why? What are you trying to hide?" I pressed.

"Nothing. I just didn't want any company."

"Why didn't you get up when we called your name and pounded on your door?" I asked as I tried to control the anger and concern that was bubbling up inside me.

"I didn't hear you."

Both of my girls were looking at Ryan and shaking their heads.

"Finish getting ready and go catch the school bus, girls. Ryan is staying home with me today. I'll call in to work and take a sick day," I said with a sigh.

Chapter 4

I watched the girls race out the door barely in time to board the school bus. Then I called in to work and left a message on the answering machine saying I was not feeling well, which was technically the truth: I was sick about the thought of Ryan messing with drugs.

Collecting myself, I returned to Ryan's bedroom to get some answers. He had lain back down on his bed and was snoring softly.

If he was really sick, I would have just let him sleep. Not this time; I wanted him wide awake and talking to me.

"Ryan, wake up," I said sternly. I wanted him to know from the sound of my voice that I meant business.

He slowly opened his eyes and looked at me.

"What did you take?" I asked.

"What are you talking about?" Ryan asked.

"What pill did you take?"

"I don't know what it was. It was supposed to help me sleep. I guess it worked, didn't it?" he said with a smirk.

"Who gave you the pill?" I probed.

"A friend."

"What friend?"

"Just a friend."

"He isn't much of a friend if he is giving an eleven-year-old boy drugs," I said.

"You're wrong, Mom."

"What did the pill look like?" I continued.

"It was a tiny white pill."

"What was it supposed to do for you?" I demanded.

"Make me sleep."

"Do you have any more?"

"No, he gave me only one. He said I would have to buy them if I wanted any more." He said his words slowly, like he had to think about each and every one of them before they crossed his lips.

"How would you get the money to buy more?" I asked.

"From you, Mom. I'll have to use my lunch money."

"I don't think so, Ryan. You won't be taking any more of those pills—or any other kind of pills. Now, get up and go take a shower. Then we will talk some more," I said sternly, hoping I was getting through the drug fog that was filling his brain.

I walked into the kitchen to get a cup of coffee. I could hear the shower, so I knew Ryan had finally done what I asked of him.

I sat and thought about what I should do about Ryan's friends. If I grounded him from going anywhere after school, I wondered how much good that would do. I wasn't always home to watch his comings and goings, and I didn't want to drop that responsibility onto his sisters.

I didn't want to ask my boss, Wayne Maxwell, what he would suggest. I didn't want him to know anything about it, to tell you the truth. He was always so critical. I guessed it was related to the fact that he was a lawyer. Anyway, seeking advice from him wasn't going to happen.

I searched my memory seeking information about some of his clients who might have had drug-related problems.

Wayne wasn't into representing druggies, so I didn't think I would be able to find any help.

I decided to call Marnie, my best friend. Because she worked at the courthouse for the commonwealth attorney, I thought she might have some information I could use to help me solve my Ryan problem.

Chapter 5

"Marnie, can you talk?" I asked.

"Yes, for a little bit. The boss is gone to court right now. Where are you? Why are you at home?" Marnie said with concern. She had recognized my home phone number, displayed on her caller ID.

"I'm home with Ryan, but I left a message at work saying I wasn't feeling well just in case someone asked you about me," I explained.

"What's wrong with Ryan?" Marnie asked.

"I'll tell you, but I don't want you to tell anyone else," I whispered into the phone.

"This sounds serious. What is it?" asked Marnie.

"My eleven-year-old son is dabbling with drugs."

"You're kidding me," Marnie said, astonished.

"I wish."

"How did you find out?"

"His eyes looked funny last night, so I started questioning him. This morning I couldn't wake him up without crawling through his bedroom window to see if he was dead. He wouldn't answer me, and he had pushed his chest of drawers against the door so we couldn't get in," I said. A hiccupping gasp escaped as I tried to quell the wave of tears that were building up inside of me.

"What did he take?" Marnie asked.

"He said it was a small white pill. He didn't know what it was," I said.

"Where did he get it?" asked Marnie.

"He said a friend gave it to him."

"Not much of a friend," commented Marnie.

"Yes, I know, but the reason I called you is to find out if you know of anyone I could talk with about what I should do next."

"You don't want to talk to anyone legal, do you?"

"No, not if it gets to social services. I don't want my ex-husband to get hold of this. He would make trouble for all of us."

"Okay, I'll do some checking and see what I can find out. Got to go, the boss is back," said Marnie as she disconnected the call.

I hung up the phone and went in search of Ryan.

The shower was no longer running, so I took that as a sign for me to continue my talk.

"Ryan, are you dressed?"

"Yeah."

I turned the doorknob and walked into the bedroom, where Ryan was stretched out on his bed completely relaxed. Immediately my anger resurfaced.

"Are you comfortable?" I asked sarcastically.

"Yeah."

"Sit up and pay attention to everything I have to say," I demanded in a tone of voice that meant business.

"Okay, okay," he snarled.

"When did you become an ugly teenager?" I asked, as I stared at him waiting for an answer.

"I'm not a teenager, yet," he snapped.

"Yes, I know. You are only eleven years old, and you have no right to be an ugly teenager because you are still a kid. Do you understand, Ryan?"

"Not really," he said sullenly.

"Let me explain, young man," I said sternly.

"Do you have to?" he asked sarcastically.

"That's exactly what I mean," I said angrily.

"What?" he asked with a puzzled look on his face.

"Your attitude is horrible. You should not be talking with me in that tone. I am your mother. You should be much more respectful. I gave you life; remember that," I blustered.

"What are you so mad about, Mom?" he asked, without any concern in his voice.

Chapter 6

How was I supposed to answer that question without going into a tirade?

I'm mad because my baby boy, my youngest child, is taking drugs.

I'm mad because I don't know how he got drawn into the drug world.

I'm mad because I didn't know it was actually happening in my neighborhood.

I was mad because I didn't know what to do to help Ryan return to being the drugless eleven-year-old boy that he should be.

"I love you, Ryan. That's why I'm so mad. I don't want you to ever take any kind of drug that isn't prescribed by your doctor. I want you to be my lovable, likeable Ryan that you were a few days ago," I said as the tears started streaming from my eyes.

Ryan finally looked at me and saw that I was crying.

"Mom, I'm so sorry that I made you cry," he said as he walked to me and put his arms around me.

"If you really are sorry, Ryan, help me get the drug dealers out of our neighborhood. You can start by giving me some names. I will take those names to someone who can track down the distributor and put a stop to the drugs," I explained as soon as the tears stopped flowing.

"They will come after me—and might even kill me. I can't tell you. They might try to kill you, Emily, and Ellen. They are dangerous people, and I'm sorry I ever got mixed up with them," Ryan said with all of the sincerity he could muster.

Studying my frightened son's face, I knew that he was telling the truth.

"Ryan, I need those names. What am I going to have to do to get you to give them to me?"

"I can't, mom."

"All right, you can't tell me, but I will find out, and I will get rid of the drugs somehow. I want you to promise me that you will never take or smoke any kind of drug off the street," I said sternly.

"I promise."

"Do you mean it? Tell me you mean what you say, Ryan," I pleaded, fighting back the waterfall of tears that were building up behind my eyes again.

"What if they make me? What am I supposed to do then?" he asked with a great deal of concern in his voice.

"Leave, just get out of there. Find some excuse to go," I blustered. "On second thought, don't go where they are. That should take care of your problem."

"I'll try."

"I need you to do more than try. You need to be clean and clear of any kind of drugs. Or..."

"Or what?"

"Or we will have to take medical or legal steps, or both, to get you going on the right path."

"You're kidding."

"Not at all. You will be clean and clear of drugs. You are my son and I love you very, very much. That is why I would take such drastic steps."

Ryan stopped talking. He knew I meant what I said.

19

Chapter 7

"Mom, after school is out, can I go out and hang around with Ronnie?"

"Is he one of your drug friends?" I asked.

"No, he's the dork who just moved in about two houses down from us. He hasn't been here long enough to know anything about the drug dealers."

"Maybe...but I really think you should spend more time at home. You've earned that as part of your punishment, don't you think?" I asked.

"Yes, I guess so," he said sullenly.

"Now, I want you to clean up your room, since you couldn't go to school."

"Aw, Mom."

"Now!"

I left the room and went to find my computer. I wanted to find the name of the DARE (Drug Abuse Resistance Education) officer in Ryan's school.

The DARE officers program was one of the greatest innovations that had been added to the school system in most of the schools. I was wondering why the drug dealers were getting in under the nose of the assigned DARE officer. Maybe they were dealing in the parking lot and bus areas. Whatever the case, it needed to be stopped.

"Ryan, do you know DARE Officer Williams?" I asked when Ryan wandered into the living room.

"Yeah."

"Do you know what he does?" I asked.

"He tells everyone to stay off drugs," he said smugly.

"You haven't been listening to him, have you?" I asked as I looked into his eyes.

"None of us listen to him because he is a cop," he said snidely.

"You're kidding me, aren't you? The DARE officer is on the school grounds to help you and anyone else who has a question about drugs," I said a bit too evenly, trying to maintain control over my temper. Ryan seemed to be pushing all of my buttons, and I was finding it very hard not to react.

"My friends avoid the DARE officer," he said solemnly, when he saw how hard I was struggling to maintain control of my tone of voice.

"You need new and different friends. A DARE officer is there to help you," I explained to ears that were not listening to me. I so much wanted to thump him on the side of his head to get him to pay attention, but barely kept myself from doing so.

I went back to the computer and delved into the subject of eleven-year-old boys and drugs.

"Well, that was disappointing," I mumbled as I moved away from the computer.

It seemed that all I could find was about the talks I should have had with him, reinforcing time and time again that he should steer clear of drugs of any kind.

I was long past the sweet talks. I needed someone to tell me what steps I should be taking next.

Chapter 8

The phone startled me with its loud interruption. I still had my landline along with my cell phone, unlike many of my friends who had disconnected their landlines, relying solely on the cellular connection. Old habits were hard to break for me.

"Hello," I said softly.

"Is Ryan there?" asked a strange voice.

"He is. Who am I speaking with?" I asked.

"A friend," said the voice.

"What friend? Tell me your name, please," I said sternly.

The strange voice responded with a 'click' followed by the blaring dial tone.

"Who was that, Mom?" asked Ryan.

"He wouldn't tell me, but he asked for you," I said curiously.

"Why didn't you let me talk to him?" asked Ryan.

"I was going to, but he hung up when I asked him his name," I explained. "Which friend of yours talks with a funny sounding voice?"

"None that I know of. What did it sound like?"

"It was definitely disguised. He didn't want me to recognize him, I think," I said, watching for Ryan's reaction. "Why would he want to hide his voice from me?"

"I don't know, Mom. I don't know who it was."

The phone rang again.

"Hello," I said.

There was another click. When I checked the caller identification, it displayed *UNAVAILABLE* and an odd telephone number.

"Ryan, come over here and look at this number. Tell me if you recognize it," I said to my son.

I saw his face blanch to white. All color had instantly drained from his cheeks.

"What's wrong, Ryan? You look like you've seen a ghost," I said worriedly.

"I recognize that phone number," he sputtered.

"Okay, who does it belong to?" I demanded.

"Someone we don't want to know," he said softly.

"And who might that be?" I demanded.

"He's the biggest drug dealer in town," whispered Ryan.

"Why is he calling you, Ryan?"

"I don't know."

"How do you even know his number?" I snapped.

"A friend of mine told me."

"What friend?" I demanded.

"I can't tell you."

This was going nowhere.

"Go to your room, Ryan. Don't come out until you are ready to talk. Do you understand?" I said angrily.

The phone rang again and I snatched it up with a gruff "Hello."

"Lindsay?"

"Oh, I'm so sorry. Hi, Marnie."

"What's wrong?" asked Marnie.

"Kids." That was all I could say.

"Now what?"

"Same old problem, an eleven-year-old boy who thinks he

is all grown up and can do anything he wants, which includes drugs," I grumbled.

"I've talked to a few people trying to find out what you can do. None of them have been very helpful, though. Most of them recommend rehab, but he is too young for that. Can you take him out of the school he's in and send him to a different one?" asked Marnie.

"If you mean a private school, no I can't afford that. If you mean a public school in another district, no I can't afford that either. I can't home school him because I have to work. Do you have any other ideas?" I asked.

"Why don't we get together and find out who the problem is? We can follow Ryan everywhere he goes, if need be," suggested Marnie.

"That sounds good to me. We have to do it soon, too. I'm getting some weird phone calls, and Ryan says they're from the big guy in the local drug dealing business. He keeps hanging up every time I answer the phone, but the first time he called, he asked for Ryan by name."

"That's not good," said Marnie.

"Yeah, I know. If I give you the phone number, can you trace it?" I asked.

"Sure, I'll slip it into one of the cases I have. I'll find out who it belongs to," said Marnie.

"Thanks. I think the phone call is only the beginning. It's just a gut feeling, but I think there's more to come," I explained in a whisper.

"What does Ryan think about the phone calls?"

"He turned as white as a sheet. I think he was really scared when he saw the number," I said.

"That's not good. I'll see what I can find out and call you back," said Marnie. I thanked her, then disconnected the line.

Chapter 9

I decided I needed to call Jed and see if he could offer me some useful advice. Even though he didn't have children of his own, he was a newspaper man; I was sure he had written about something related to the business of drugs, or know someone who did.

"Hey, Jed," I greeted him softly.

"Hi, Linds, what's up?" he replied as usual.

"Well, I've got a problem and I'm looking for help. I hope you have some answers for me. I could really use some help," I said with a sigh.

"Tell me what's going on," Jed said, concern apparent in his voice.

Jed and I had been friends for a few years. We got to know each other when he called me to find out if there was anything newsworthy in my little town because he was a feature writer looking for a story. My name had been given to him by the writer he had replaced.

"It's drugs, and Ryan has become involved with them," I said, in a husky tone caused by the tears building up.

"*Ryan?* But he's just a little kid," Jed said incredulously.

"I know, I know. I couldn't believe it either, at first," I said softly.

"How did that happen?" he asked.

"I'm trying to find that out. Ryan won't talk about it. He is too afraid to tell me anything. He isn't afraid of me so much; it's the drug dealers that scare him," I said, as the tears started to roll down my cheeks.

"Do you want me to come over and talk to Ryan?" he asked.

"Yes and no. He probably won't hear a word you say, but he will sit there while you talk. But I could use any help I could get," I said sincerely.

"I'll be there in about an hour. This sounds like a good story for me to check out," he said.

"I'm not telling you about this to get it in the newspaper. That's way too dangerous for Ryan and the rest of us. Please don't write about it," I begged.

"What do you mean? How can it be dangerous to your family?" he demanded.

"Ryan said if he talked, they would kill him—and maybe Ellen, Emily, and me as well. If this gets into the newspaper, that might happen to all of us. You might be included because you wrote the story," I explained.

"Don't worry, Lindsay, I won't name names if that's a problem," he said hurriedly. "I'll be there soon, okay?"

"Okay. I could use the moral support. My backbone seems to be slipping, and I don't know what to do next," I said, feeling a sudden surge of imminent tears.

The call ended and I broke down into a mountain of sobs. I loved my son so much, and I didn't want him to be in any kind of trouble. I definitely didn't want him to die.

Ellen and Emily bounded inside when they climbed off of the school bus. I was glad to see them rush back into my life.

"Mom, where was Ryan sneaking off to?" asked Ellen.

"Nowhere. He is supposed to be in his bedroom," I said, exasperated.

"Well, he isn't. I saw him walking off with one of the older kids from school," Ellen shot back.

"Ryan...*Ryan!*" I shouted.

No answer.

Running to his bedroom, I opened the door. Heart sinking, I saw his open window and knew he was gone.

I ran back to the front door, opened it, and peered outside looking for my missing son.

"Do you know who he was walking with?" I asked Ellen.

"I don't know his name, but he goes to the high school," she answered.

"Emily, do you know the guy?" I asked.

"Like Ellen said, he goes to the high school. He isn't in any of my classes, and I don't know his name either," she replied.

"Why would a high school kid be hanging around with a kid in middle school?" I asked my daughters.

My only answer from them was a shrug.

"Does that kid have a reputation for selling drugs or doing drugs?" I asked them

Again, I got the shrugs. I knew I had to dig deeper.

"I don't understand shrugs. I need words, girls. I need answers, *now*," I said sternly.

"Don't get mad at us, Mom. We didn't do anything. Ryan did, not us," Emily said in defense of her sister and herself.

"Tell me more about the young man who was with Ryan," I said firmly.

Chapter 10

I went to Ryan's room hoping to find some kind of hint as to where he took off to when he was supposed to be grounded. I stuck my head out of the open window looking for a sign, any sign, that would tell me the direction that he took toward trouble.

Nothing appeared helpful; there was not even flattened grass to show me a sign Ryan had been there. I went back to the living room just as Jed arrived at my front door.

"Come on in," I shouted.

"Linds. What's happening?" he asked too cheerfully.

The happiness on his face stomped on my one last nerve.

"Nothing to be happy about," I snapped. "I have a missing son, and I hope he didn't go to join the druggies who have been talking to him."

"Chill out, Lindsay. I'm here to help you find him. The happiness is that I'm glad to see you again," explained Jed as he forced a frown to his face.

"I'm sorry, Jed. I'm just so worried about him, and angry with him on top of that. I really didn't mean to snap at you."

"What are you planning to do to find him?" Jed asked.

"I don't know. Maybe ride around in the neighborhood? Maybe we can spot him walking around," I said hopefully.

"Let's go. I'll drive so you can look," said Jed.

I grabbed my handbag and headed for the door. The girls were in their rooms, so I didn't have to worry too much about them. I just turned and yelled down the hallway, telling them Jed and I were looking for Ryan.

"Which way?" asked Jed after we were both settled in his car.

"Left, toward town. I think that's where we can find the drug dealers," I answered. As we rolled along, I strained to see as far as I could down the road.

"Slow down, Jed."

"Do you see him?" he asked.

"No, but if you drive too fast, I can't see anything. The people all become a blur," I explained.

"Okay. That's not a problem with me, but I think the people behind me might not like it," he said, glancing to the rearview mirror.

"Tough," I said. I continued to scan both sides of the street.

Jed drove slowly through town, then turned, and went back so I could get a better view of the other side of the street.

"I don't see any kids out and about," I said, as I continued to scan the street.

"They shouldn't be out. They should be at home, eating dinner or doing homework," said Jed. We crept along for several more blocks, much to the dismay of those drivers behind us.

"Well, he isn't out walking around. If he was, we would have seen him already. Where else should we go?" asked Jed.

"Let's cruise through the neighborhood. It's away from town, and kids wouldn't be afraid to be outside with their buddies," I said.

"Sure, that's a good idea," Jed responded as he turned onto my street.

He circled the block and then moved out farther, making the circle much wider.

"Over there?" I said, pointing out the windshield.

"Is that him?" asked Jed.

"I can't be sure until we get a little closer," I answered excitedly.

Jed stepped on the gas pedal, and we were instantly much closer.

"Ryan!" I shouted at a figure running in the opposite direction. "Ryan! Stop running!" He disappeared behind an outbuilding in an area where Jed couldn't drive his car without doing damage to the undercarriage.

Chapter 11

"Stop the car, Jed. I need to go back there to find Ryan," I said hurriedly.

I jumped out of the vehicle before the car came to a stop and took off running towards the area where Ryan had disappeared.

"Linds, slow down!" Jed shouted.

"I can't! I've got to find Ryan!" I shouted back at him. Then I, too, disappeared from Jed's sight.

I ran as fast as I could toward the small figure that was running away from me. The rabbiting form didn't hesitate at the shout and was rapidly moving farther away from me.

"Oh, God, no. Don't disappear. Please slow down," I prayed as I ran at a slower pace. I couldn't go any further. I had to stop and catch my breath. A moment later, Jed caught up with me.

"Where did he go?" he asked.

I pointed forward and shrugged as I continued to breathe heavily.

"Are you sure it was Ryan?" he asked.

Again, I shrugged.

"It looked like him, but I was so far away I couldn't be sure," I said.

"Let's go back to the car and continue looking," suggested Jed.

"Where?" I asked. Once again, I fought the onslaught of tears.

Jed put his arms around me and held me close. I really needed his strength; at that moment, for an instant, it was all I needed and wanted.

He released me and we started walking back to the car.

"We'll find him, Lindsay," he said, when I started to open the car door.

"I hope it isn't too late," I added solemnly.

"What do you mean by 'too late?'" asked Jed.

"I hope they don't get him hooked on drugs. That's what I mean," I said angrily.

"He's your son. You aren't giving him enough credit," said Jed.

"But he told me he had taken some drugs. Maybe he shouldn't get that much credit," I retorted.

We were on the road again, but there was no more sign of Ryan.

"We should go on to the house. Maybe he'll come home. I would hate to call the police and report him as a runaway," I said.

Jed and I walked into the house, and there he was in all of his glory.

Chapter 12

"Why are you sitting here? Where have you been?" I demanded.

"I had things to do," he replied smugly.

"Where *were* you?" I growled, trying to rein in my anger at his remark.

"You didn't want me to hang out with my friends anymore, so I had to tell them," Ryan explained.

"How did they take it?" asked Jed.

"Not good. I had to run to get away from them, but they know where I live," Ryan said timidly.

"Do you think they'll hurt you?" asked Jed while I looked on.

"I think they'll hurt all of us. They are not nice people," said Ryan.

"How?" I asked when I finally grasped in my mind what he was saying.

"Anything they can do and get away with." Ryan said softly.

"Like what?" I asked.

"Fires, car accidents, stuff like that. They want whatever they do to be something they can't be blamed for doing," Ryan answered.

"How did you get involved with these people?" I asked.

"At school. Some of them were my classmates. I thought they were good people. But boy, was I wrong, about everyone except Devon. I think he was drawn into this mess just like I was. He wants out, too, but they said they would kill him. So he had to stay."

"What are we supposed to do now, Ryan?" I demanded.

My little boy finally returned to me when he burst into tears and reached to me for comfort.

"Jed, do you have any suggestions?" I asked as I held onto Ryan.

"You need to let the cops know what is happening or about to happen, so that they can get some extra patrols going on this street. Ryan will need to give them some names so they can do some background checks and possibly pull some of the gang in for questioning," he said solemnly.

"You can't get the cops involved. They'll kill me," pleaded Ryan.

"Ryan, listen to me," I said. I pushed him away from my body, forcing him to release the clutch he had on me. "We have to have their help if we want to get through this mess."

"No! No, they will kill all of us!" Ryan wailed tearfully. He was shaking and I could tell he was on the verge of hysterics.

"Settle down, Ryan. You know we can't do this alone. We have to have some kind of help. I don't think we should call them to come to the house, especially if we are being watched. We all need to go meet an undercover officer, maybe at a restaurant somewhere, if they will do that for us," I suggested.

"What about the girls?" asked Jed.

"We will have to tell them all about this. For that matter, where are they?" I asked, when I realized I had not heard from them for a while.

"Ellen, Emily," I shouted from the hallway outside of their closed bedroom doors.

There was no response from either of the two bedrooms.

My patience was wearing thin.

"El, Em, front and center right now!" I screamed.

I jerked Ellen's bedroom door open and the place was empty. I ran to Emily's door and yanked it open to find it empty as well.

"Jed, look on the fridge. See if they left me a note," I said.

"No, there's no note."

"Ryan, were the girls here when you came home?" I asked.

"I didn't see them, but I didn't look for them," he answered.

"Do you know where they might be?" I asked Ryan.

"Maybe," he said sadly.

"All right, where?" I demanded.

"They might have taken my sisters as a punishment for me," he said in a barely audible tone.

"You've got to be kidding me!" I shouted.

"I don't know for sure, but they might have taken my sisters before I got back to the house," he muttered.

"Ryan, what have you done?" I asked in total exasperation.

Chapter 13

"I'm going to check to see if they have their IDs with them. They know not to go anywhere without some form of identification," I said, walking into Emily's room.

"Oh, no, it's here. Em doesn't have her ID with her," I said as I walked toward Ellen's room, where I discovered her ID laying on her dresser. I sat down on Ellen's bed, gazing at her walls filled with her most special memories.

"Ryan, where would they have taken Emily and Ellen?" I demanded as soon as I returned to the living room.

"To the meeting cabin," he replied.

"Where would that be?" I asked, trying to control my tone of voice.

"I can't tell you. I was sworn to secrecy," he muttered.

"You *what*?!" I screeched. No voice control was possible this time.

"It was a blood oath. I can't tell anyone," he mumbled.

"You *will* tell me, Ryan. Now, spill it," I demanded.

"I'll have to show you," he whispered.

"Okay, let's all get in the car, right now. Ryan is going to show us where the girls might have been taken," I told Jed hurriedly, grabbing my handbag and car keys.

I drove with Jed in the front passenger seat while Ryan rode in the back so he could duck down and hide from view. At least, that was what he told me.

"Okay, Ryan, we're on Main Street. Now where do we go?" I asked. I glanced into the rearview mirror to get a look at him.

"Just keep driving until you get to the Frog Level turn off. Then you take a right on the first gravel road you see," he said softly.

"That's quite a ways from the house; how did you get to the meeting cabin?" I asked.

"On my bike," he answered.

I wanted to scold him for riding his bike that far from home, but what was the use? It was too late to get into that problem when we had bigger hurdles ahead.

"Is that the road, Ryan?" I asked as I slowed the car down to a crawl.

"Yes, but if you drive up there, they will probably shoot you," he said in a frightened tone.

"Should we get out and walk?" I asked skeptically.

"Yes, but park the car on the other road so they won't know where you're going."

"How far do we have to walk?" I asked, dubious again.

"It's not too far. But I'm going to stay in the car, if you don't care?" he said in a pleading tone.

"I do care, and you're not staying in the car. You are coming with Jed and me. I don't want to lose you, too," I said sternly.

I parked the car on the shoulder of the paved road and we all got out to start walking.

"Ryan, you lead the way," I said as I gave him a little shove forward.

"No! I don't want to lead," he sputtered.

"That's too bad," I said. "Now lead."

Ryan tried to hang back behind Jed and me, but I pushed him forward.

"Mom, stop it," he whimpered.

"How much farther, Ryan?" I asked in a harsh whisper.

"Over there," he said, pointing off to his right.

"I don't see a meeting cabin or clubhouse of any kind," I snapped.

"It's behind those trees," he mumbled.

A shot rang out and whizzed past my ear.

"I told you they would shoot," said Ryan sarcastically.

"Run to the car!" I said as I took off running.

I hit the button to unlock the car doors and we all jumped in without looking back.

"That's it!" I said. "Now it's time to talk to the police."

Chapter 14

I guided my car back into town and pulled into the police department parking lot.

"Mom, they will kill us," said Ryan in a tear-filled whisper.

"That's what I'm trying to prevent. Get out of the car now, and tell the police everything you know," I said sternly,

Ryan scooted to the other side of the back seat to let me know that he wasn't about to crawl out.

"Get over here now, Ryan. You don't want me to crawl in there to get a hold of you, do you?" I asked harshly.

"Mom, I can't," he whimpered.

"You can and you will," I said in a softer tone, then grabbed for any part of his body that I could reach.

"Please don't make me go," he pleaded.

I managed to reach a foot and I gave it a quick jerk.

"Let's go!"

At that point, he knew he didn't have a choice so he crawled out slowly. As soon as his feet hit the ground, I knew I would have to physically push him every step toward the door to enter the police station.

Once inside, I spoke with the clerk and specifically asked to speak with a narcotics detective.

Because I was so specific, I knew we would have to wait until someone became available.

We sat on a hard wooden bench opposite the check-in desk for more than an hour. When Ryan became fidgety, I sent him to the men's restroom to hide from being on public display.

Eventually, a tall thin man with stern features introduced himself as Detective Mark Wilson.

"Jed, go get Ryan out of the men's restroom," I whispered.

Jed hurried off and I introduced myself to the detective.

"I'm Lindsay Harris, and someone took a shot at the three of us," I said, pointing to Ryan and Jed who had emerged from the men's restroom.

"Where did this take place?"

"Off Route Sixteen, just past the Frog Level turnoff," I answered.

"Do you know who pulled the trigger?" proved the detective.

"No, I don't—but he does," I said, as I pointed to Ryan. He was trying to hide behind Jed.

"Are you pointing at the kid, or the man he's hiding behind?" asked Detective Wilson.

"The kid, and his name is Ryan."

"Okay Ryan, what's going on?" asked Detective Wilson

Ryan didn't want to answer, but I tapped him on the shoulder and said, "Speak up."

"I think it was one of my friends, not Devon, who took a shot at us," he mumbled.

"Why would you think it was friend?" the detective probed.

"Because we were getting close to the cabin, and my friends would not allow that," Ryan said, a little bit louder.

"Why would that matter?" asked Detective Wilson.

"It's a secret clubhouse. Only members are allowed," explained Ryan.

"What kind of club to you belong to that is so secretive?"

asked the detective.

"Just a bunch of guys," said Ryan as he squirmed in his seat.

"Tell him, Ryan," I snapped, glaring at my squirming son.

"Drugs," he mumbled.

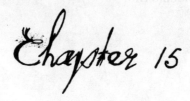

Chapter 15

Detective Mark Wilson was totally interested in our plight right after the utterance of the word *drugs*.

"Are you directly involved with the sale and distribution of any kind of drugs?" asked the detective.

"No, sir. Devon and I are new to the club, so we weren't given any of those duties," Ryan answered.

"Who is Devon?" asked the detective.

"My best friend," answered Ryan.

"What did you do for them?" he probed.

"Mostly cleaning up. We had to earn the right to be a regular club member," Ryan answered.

"How long was that going to take?" probed the detective.

"I don't know. They never did tell me," Ryan said solemnly.

"What are the names of the club members?" the detective asked.

Ryan cast his glance to the floor, shuffled his feet, and sighed.

"Come on, Ryan, tell me those names," urged the detective.

"I can't," mumbled Ryan.

"Young man, you are already in a lot of trouble. Keeping those names from me will not help," Detective Wilson said sternly.

"I really don't know their actual names. I know only their club names," said Ryan.

"Let's start with those," directed the detective.

Ryan, again, cast his glance to the floor and shuffled his feet.

"If I tell you, they will kill me and my family," he said as he fought back the tears that were forcing their way into his eyes.

"We won't let that happen," said the detective.

"How are you going to do that?" asked Ryan, wiping at his tears.

"Yes, I would like to know that myself," I added.

My interruption to his conversation must have caught the detective off guard for a moment. He glared at me and said, "We can patrol your street more often."

"That won't do anything to help us," I said sarcastically. "We could be killed between patrols."

"Ma'am, we don't have the manpower to babysit you," he snapped.

"Then my son doesn't have the time or the energy to give you any names. I'm afraid he might be suffering from a memory lapse."

Ryan suddenly sat up straighter and looked at me. He wasn't expecting that kind of reaction from me.

"Ma'am, your son is in a lot of trouble," stammered the detective.

"No, he isn't; not legally, not yet. We came here to report a shooting and nothing else. Now, we are leaving, and you can go to blazes before we offer to help you again," I said angrily as I stood up to leave. Jed and Ryan both stood, and we turned to leave the office.

"You folks need to slow down," said the detective. "Maybe we can talk about this."

"I don't think we can, if you are going to continually threaten my son. We are all under a serious threat for our lives as it is," I said in a controlled, even tone. I turned and left his office with Jed and Ryan close behind me.

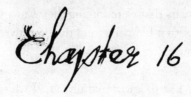

Chapter 16

When we climbed into the car, I breathed a sigh of relief. "Well, that was a wasted effort," I told Jed.

"No, not really... Now they know that if something happens to us, they can look to the club for some answers," suggested Jed.

"By that time, it will be too late," said Ryan from his hiding place in the back seat.

"That's a good possibility if you don't plan to talk. I didn't get a chance to tell them about Ellen and Emily being missing," I said to Ryan.

At just about the moment my mouth closed, my car was slammed into by another vehicle that didn't bother to stop. The collision point was on the passenger side in the rear.

As soon as my scrambled brain would allow me to form sentences, I turned to check on Ryan and Jed.

"Ryan, are you okay?" I asked, struggling to look at him.

No response.

"Ryan, answer me!" I shouted.

"He's not moving," mumbled Jed as he tried to remove his seat belt.

"Are you all right, Jed?" I asked.

"Yes, but call nine-one-one for Ryan," he answered.

My cell phone had fallen to the floor, and I had to scoot around and grope to find it.

"Here it is," I said. I tried to focus my eyes on the keypad.

"Nine-one-one, what is your emergency?" asked a professional voice.

"I'm in the police station parking lot and my car was hit, hurting my son. He is unconscious and we need an ambulance."

Suddenly there were many uniformed bodies surrounding my car. One of the bodies jerked the car door open to see Ryan sprawled out on the back seat, totally unaware of his surroundings.

They lifted him out of the car and placed him on the cot that had mysteriously appeared.

"Where are you taking him?" I asked anxiously, still in the driver's seat. I had not been able to manipulate the complexity of releasing my seat belt.

"To Mercy Hospital, about a mile down the road. Are you his mother?" asked a concerned EMT.

"Yes sir."

"You can get in back and ride with him."

"Thank you, thank you," I mumbled after finally releasing myself from my car seat restraint.

I looked around to find Jed.

"Can you stay with the car and ask them to call Detective Wilson?" I asked, climbing into the back of the ambulance.

Jed rubbed the back of his neck as he answered, "Sure. I'll meet you at the hospital."

"Do you need to go to the emergency room?" I asked.

"No, I don't think so. I'll find you after I talk to Wilson," he answered.

Chapter 17

The trip to the hospital was short, and the EMTs continued trying to rouse Ryan. They whisked him into the emergency room, where a crowd of doctors and nurses surrounded him.

A strong-armed nurse grabbed me and shuffled me out of the emergency room into a waiting room.

"We will let you know when he wakes up," she said, then walked away back into the cavernous emergency room.

I collapsed onto a chair and sobbed.

"My God," I prayed. "Why is this happening to us?"

A few moments later, I was being picked up from the floor of the waiting room. I was placed into a wheelchair and pushed into the emergency room where I, too, was surrounded by medical personnel.

"I'm all right," I mumbled as I was undressed and told to climb onto the cot so they could check me over completely. "Is my son okay?"

"He is right next to you," said the nurse in a soothing voice.

"You didn't answer my question. Is he all right?" I demanded loudly.

"I will check on him and tell you if you promise to relax and let the doctors help you," said the patient nurse. She gave me a comforting pat on the shoulder.

The patting didn't help, but the doctor was asking me questions and my mind was diverted from Ryan for a short time.

Because I had been found sprawled out on the waiting room floor after having endured an automobile collision, the doctor wanted x-rays taken of my neck and head to find the reason for the unconsciousness.

When the doctor disappeared from my curtained cubicle, my focus once again shifted to Ryan.

"How is my son?" I asked the nurse, who had returned to my cubicle as soon as the doctor exited on his way to write the orders for my x-rays.

"He is still unconscious, but he is showing signs of coming to the surface," the nurse explained.

"What does that mean?" I asked.

"He is not as deep into the coma as he was. He is trying to return to you, and that's a really good sign," the nurse said as she checked my readings on the monitor.

The orderly entered the cubicle to usher me to x-ray for pictures.

I was getting impatient with all of this attention because I wanted to see my son.

Because I was considered an emergency, the x-ray technician was fast and gentle with me. I was returned to my cubicle in emergency to await the results.

"How is my son doing?" I asked the nurse.

"Still the same," she replied.

Of course I didn't want to hear that answer, but there was nothing I could do except wait. Waiting was not one of my strengths; impatience overrode the waiting every time.

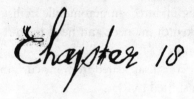

Chapter 18

Sounds of activity emanated from the cubicle where Ryan was stationed.

"What's happening to my son?!" I shouted.

The nurse who had left a moment before rushed back in and stood beside my bed.

"They are taking your son to ICU so he can be monitored constantly for signs of improvement," she whispered.

"When will the doctor be back in here? I need to go to ICU with my son," I said as I started to climb down off of the bed.

"Whoa, hold on! Wait, Ms. Harris. I will check with the doctor if you climb back onto the bed, please," urged the nurse as she gently pushed me up a bit to settle myself on the bed.

I lay back on the bed and all became dark inside my head.

I had no idea how long I was out, but when I surfaced, I was once again surrounded by medical personnel.

"Ms. Harris," said a soft masculine voice, "I'm Dr. Maloney."

I blinked my eyes several times as I tried to focus in on the man who was speaking.

"What was your name, again?" I asked when I could finally see his face.

"Dr. Maloney," he said in response.

"What's happening to me?" I asked.

"You've injured your neck, and it's causing you to disconnect from your brain. You will need to wear a brace for a while, keeping the sudden movements to your neck at a bare minimum so the connection can heal," he explained.

"Can I get out of here soon? Please? I have a son in ICU and I need to check on him," I pleaded.

"Do you have someone to drive you home?" asked the nurse who was standing next to the doctor.

"I'm not sure if he has arrived yet," I said.

"There is a gentleman in the waiting room asking about you. I will send him in," said the nurse.

"His name is Jed," I said. She nodded as she left the curtained cubicle.

Jed was led to my bedside, and he was followed by Detective Wilson.

"How are you, Linds?" asked Jed.

"I'm okay. I'm just going to have to wear a brace for a while so I won't black out," I answered.

"How is Ryan?" Jed asked appearing concerned.

"He's in ICU. I need to go there as soon as I get fitted with the brace," I said. "Is my car drivable?"

"Yes, it's here in the parking lot—but Detective Wilson needs to talk with you. I told him about your missing daughters," said Jed in almost a whisper.

"Ms. Harris, did you see the person who hit your car?" asked the detective.

"No, sir. My car was parked and standing still, so I wasn't looking behind me at the time. I was just getting situated so I could leave," I answered calmly.

"Your friend didn't see anyone either. Your son is in no condition to talk," said the puzzled detective.

"My son was hiding from sight, so I'm sure he didn't see anything," I added.

"Mr. Thompson said your daughters are missing. When did that happen?" probed Detective Wilson.

"While we were out looking for Ryan earlier this afternoon. What time is it now? I've lost my conception of time because I kept passing out," I answered truthfully.

"It's six o'clock," said Jed.

"Oh my gosh! I've been here way too long. I need to check on Ryan and go hunt for my girls," I said as I tried to get out of bed.

The lights in my head went out again, but I woke up quickly this time.

"Stay there until you get that brace. Detective Wilson and I will look for the girls. I'll check on Ryan, too, and call you," he said. He handed me the cellphone he had removed from the car.

Chapter 19

Waiting...I was waiting still for them to fit me with that brace so I wouldn't pass out.

Finally fitted with the brace, I was allowed to leave with the assistance of Jed. Detective Wilson was in tow as I asked them to take me to ICU to check on Ryan. That would eliminate the need for Jed to call me and report in. I wanted to see Ryan for myself.

"There's been no change. Perhaps you should go on home, and we will call you when things do change," said a polite but professional nurse. She was stationed at the desk in front of the monitor, where she could see Ryan at all times. Looking into the area where Ryan's bed was positioned, I saw all kinds of lines hooked up to various parts of his small body. I cringed when I saw the display.

"You will call?" I asked.

"Yes ma'am. You are his mother?" she asked.

I nodded and forced my tears to go away, blinking rapidly.

Jed pushed me in my wheelchair out to the lobby, and told me to wait while he pulled the car up to the front entrance.

Detective Wilson waited with me and started asking more questions.

"Who do you think took your daughters?"

"The same people who hit my car," I said sullenly. "Also, the same people that took a shot at us."

"I need to know who they are. Do you have any idea?" he asked sheepishly.

"No, all I can tell you is the location of their clubhouse. That's where the shooting occurred," I said.

"Okay, Ms. Harris, I'll get a SWAT Team to check out that clubhouse. I will also fill out a missing person report for your daughters. We will be doing everything we can to locate your daughters, and protect you and your son from any further danger," he said apologetically.

The phrase that popped into my mind was *better late than never*, but I held my tongue long enough to whisper, "Thank you, Detective Wilson."

Jed drove me home to an empty house where all I could do was cry. I was miserable, with the brace not allowing me to move my head. If I wanted to look to the side, I had to turn my whole body.

While I was sitting on the sofa feeling sorry for myself, there was a knock on my front door.

Chapter 20

"Stay there. I'll get it," said Jed. As he was reaching for the doorknob, he paused. Jed was apprehensive about opening the door without knowing who was on the other side.

"Who is it?" he said loudly.

There was a barely audile mumble from the visitor. Jed was unable to understand what was being said.

"Speak up! I can't hear you," Jed shouted.

Mumbling again.

"I'm not going to open the door until you tell me who you are," Jed shouted angrily. He stepped to the side, thinking he might distinguish the mumbling a little better.

A shot came crashing through the center of the door, and it would have hit Jed in the chest if he hadn't stepped to the side.

"Dial nine-one-one, Linds," he said in a harsh whisper. "Get behind the sofa to do it so you won't get shot."

I rose from the sofa slowly because the neck brace forced me to make slow movements. I pulled the sofa from the wall, then got down on my knees because that was all I could do.

"Help, please, someone just fired a shot through my front door. My name is Lindsay Harris, and Detective Mark Wilson is working on my case," I said hurriedly.

"A car is on its way to you, and I will notify Detective Wilson. Is the shooter still there?" asked the 9-1-1 operator.

"I don't know," I answered with a shaky voice.

"Ma'am, stay on the phone with me until the police arrive. Okay?" asked the operator.

"I'll try," I answered softly.

Jed was hiding behind a chair that was nowhere near the door.

"The police are on the way," I said softly.

"I hear the sirens now," responded Jed.

"Do you hear the shooter anymore?" I asked.

"They probably left when the sirens started," replied Jed. "At least, I hope they did. I really wouldn't want any more bullets flying outside your front door. It's becoming really dangerous to be around you and your family," he said with a shaky smile.

"Leave, if you feel that way about us," I said petulantly.

"You know I wouldn't do that," said Jed.

"I know," I said, as the tears started to fill my eyes.

"Police!" was shouted and the door was pushed open.

Chapter 21

The policemen rushed in with guns drawn. I raised my hands, as did Jed.

"I'm the one who called you," I shouted.

"I'm with her," said Jed defensively.

One of the officers pulled out pencil and notepad. He poised himself to take notes.

"Tell me what happened here," he said authoritatively.

"Well," I said, just as authoritatively, "Someone shot at us through my front door."

He glanced at the door, noticing the large hole.

"Who did that?" he asked.

"I don't know. That's why I called you. I need your help! This is the second time I've been shot at, not to mention that someone smashed into my car in the police station parking lot."

"You're the lady that Mark Wilson is trying to help," he said in astonishment.

"His help is not doing much to stop this," I said sullenly.

The officer looked for the bullet that had caused the hole. It was located in the plaster of the wall opposite the door. After photographing the hole in the door and the final resting place of the bullet, he started asking me questions.

I told them to talk to Detective Wilson.

"I need some information for my report right now," he said in a huff.

"Okay, I'm Lindsay Harris and this is Jed Thompson," I said, pointing to him. "We just got home from the hospital where my son is in Intensive Care because of the accident at the police station parking lot. There was a knock at the door, and when we didn't open it without questioning who was on the other side, the bullet came flying through the door."

"You didn't see who did this?" asked the officer.

"No sir, we didn't open the door," I said again. "We didn't see the shooter."

"Do you have any idea who would have done this?" he asked.

"It's the same people who shot at us the first time and hit my car. They are determined to kill my whole family," I said as I fought the tears again. "They also have kidnapped my two daughters. Please find them."

"How are you involved in this?" the officer asked Jed.

"I'm a friend of the family, and I have been present at all three incidents," Jed answered.

"Do you think the aggression might be directed towards you, Mr. Thompson?" probed the officer.

"No sir, I didn't have a problem until I came here. I live in a different town."

"Maybe you should go back home," suggested the officer.

"I don't think so. Not until I help Lindsay get her girls back—which is something you should be doing, don't you think?" Jed said, his attitude showing a bit.

"Perhaps you're right, Mr. Thompson, but we have to deal with this situation at the moment," said the officer politely, in an effort to calm Jed's obvious anger.

"Come sit beside me, Jed, while the officers finish up," I said, trying to diffuse Jed's building temper as well as my own.

Chapter 22

Jed and I looked around to find something to cover the hole in the door. We ended up taping cardboard over it until I was able to purchase and install a new door.

The telephone started ringing and I carefully rose from my spot on the sofa to try to grab it before it stopped.

"Hello," I said softly into the receiver.

"Mom?"

"Emily? Is that you?" I asked excitedly.

"Mom. Can you come get us?" asked a frightened voice.

"Is that you, Emily?" I sputtered. "Where are you?"

"Mom, help us," said the voice.

"Who is this?" I demanded.

"Mom, help us," said the voice.

"Why are you doing this to me?" I cried.

Silence.

"Who would do such a mean thing?" I asked Jed as I placed the receiver back onto its cradle.

"The same people who are holding the girls. They are trying to rattle you some more," he answered.

"Well, they are doing an excellent job," I stammered.

"Did that sound like Emily?" Jed asked.

"Yes and no," I answered slowly as I thought about the voice. "It might have been her, but the whole conversation sounded recorded. She wasn't answering any of my questions."

"Then you aren't sure it was Emily, are you?" asked Jed.

"No, I'm not sure, but it did sound a bit like her."

"I think you need to let the cops find the girls," said Jed. "Don't pay any mind to what they say on the phone except to report it to the legal authorities. Maybe you should call Detective Wilson now and let him know that they called you and are harassing you."

"I guess you're right, I'm just so worried."

"I know you are."

As I reached for the telephone to dial the police station, the instrument started to ring again. My nerves were so strained I jumped at the sound.

"Hello," I said as I tried to calm myself.

"Ms. Harris, this is Detective Wilson. Do you have a few moments to speak with me?" he asked politely.

"Yes, Detective Wilson. I was just going to call you."

"What were you calling about? Did you discover something new on the whereabouts of your daughters?" he asked with evident interest.

"I received a telephone call a few minutes ago from someone who sounded like Emily," I started.

"Was it Emily?"

"I'm not sure. I think the words I heard were pre-recorded. The one talking didn't answer any of my questions. I just didn't feel good about the whole conversation," I said solemnly.

"We will try to trace the call back to its origins, with your permission," said the detective.

"Yes, please, I'll let you do anything that will help find my babies," I said, fighting the tears that were rising to the surface.

"I wanted you to know that the clubhouse was searched, but

unfortunately, it had been abandoned. We have gathered some pieces of evidence, but it will take several days to get it all processed."

"I was afraid that would happen. You have no clue where they would be. You have no clue where they would have packed up and moved to, do you?" I asked.

"No, Ms. Harris, but we have feelers out for people to let us know if any unusual gatherings occur. We will find them, and your daughters. That is a promise," he said solemnly.

"Thank you, Detective Wilson," I said as he mumbled a quick goodbye.

Chapter 23

"Jed, I need to go back to the hospital to check on Ryan," I said in a pleading tone.

"They said they would call you if there was any change," he reminded me.

"I know, but I really need to see for myself," I said sadly.

"Okay, I guess you're not going to be happy until we go," he said. He helped me rise awkwardly from the sofa. The neck brace was getting to be a painful hindrance.

I saw a police car parked across the street from my house, so I asked Jed to tell him we were going to the hospital to check on Ryan.

"He's going to follow us," said Jed when he returned.

We took Jed's car so that whoever was after me and mine wouldn't be able to pick us out in a crowd.

Well, I was wrong about that.

We went inside to go to ICU for an update on Ryan's condition. I heard the same old phrases: *no change* and *we will call you*; so we made our way back to Jed's car—where we found four flat tires.

I wondered how that had happened if the police officer who had followed us was still sitting in his car. Turning carefully to look, I saw he wasn't there. He was gone, probably called away for another incident.

Again, I called 9-1-1 to report the problem. I asked them to have Detective Wilson give me a call and send somebody out to investigate the flat tires incident.

I called a local car repair shop who sent out a flatbed truck to haul Jed's SUV into the shop for new tires.

I stayed at the hospital to be near Ryan, while Jed went with his vehicle to take care of the expenses.

Jed refused to use my debit car to pay for the tires. He said he would be reimbursed by his insurance company, or so he thought.

"Ms. Harris, your son is beginning to wake up," whispered the nurse who entered the room where I was sitting to wait for Jed's return.

I slowly rose from my seat to follow the nurse. When we reached the entrance to ICU, we were prevented from entering the area by a security guard.

"I need some identification," said the guard, as I stood and stared at him.

I fumbled around in my handbag until I found my driver's license.

"Why are you doing this?" I asked when I handed him my identification.

"The hospital received a threat," he explained.

"What kind of a threat?" I asked anxiously. "My son is in ICU."

"Yes ma'am. The threat was specifically against ICU and your son."

"Do you know who made the threat?" I asked. I needed to know why this was happening.

"It was made anonymously," he said as he shrugged his shoulders.

"Isn't there any way to find out?" I demanded.

"It's being followed up by the investigators. That takes time," he said as he opened the door for me to enter ICU.

"Tell me about it," I mumbled as I walked past him.

I took a quick glance at Ryan, but I didn't see any change. Perhaps the medical people noticed it in the instruments that were recording his every breath.

I stood around for a while, staring at the monitors, but I could see no change. I watched my son as the machine breathed for him. There were hoses and tubes attached to every orifice as well as several new openings that had been made to accommodate blood infusion. It was so scary to see. I wondered if he would ever wake up and if he did, if he would be the same boy.

Chapter 24

The return of Jed caused me to rise up and start fighting no matter what the cost.

"Jed, we need to find the girls. We can't do anything to help Ryan right now, but we can go look for my daughters. Are you game?"

"Of course I'm game. Where do you think we should start?" he asked with an encouraging smile.

"Let's go out to where their old hangout used to be. We'll kick over a few rocks to see what we can find," I said.

I really didn't expect to find anything at their former clubhouse, but I thought we should at the very least give it a try.

I was smiling when we arrived at our destination.

"What's up with the smile?" asked Jed.

"I was just thinking how nice it would be to find something the police had overlooked," I answered.

"That's not very likely," said Jed.

"I know, but it is a good thought," I said. My smile remained in place.

We climbed out of Jed's SUV slowly, checking all around us for the possibility that the gang had returned. It was eerily quiet. The birds were silent, and there were no rustling sounds in the underbrush.

"It sure is quiet," whispered Jed.

"Too quiet," I whispered in return.

"Stay close, Linds. This place makes me nervous," Jed said as he kept turning his head from side to side to check out the area.

We moved in closer to the clubhouse with the thought of going inside. When we arrived at the door, we saw the crime scene seal that had been placed across the door facing. The tape was hanging down and blowing in the breeze, so we knew someone had already checked the place out after the police left and before we arrived.

"That's not a good sign," Jed said, pointing to the dangling crime scene tape.

"I still want to go inside to take a look," I said. My smile had completely disappeared.

Jed reached toward the doorknob and paused.

"Are you sure you want to do this?" he asked.

"Yes, I am. What's the problem?"

"There's a bad smell coming from in there."

I stepped up closer to the door and got a whiff of the odor.

"What is that?" I asked as I raised my hand to cover my mouth.

"Let's hope it is a dead animal and not a dead human being," said Jed. He, too, covered his mouth and nose.

Jed pushed the door and winced from the overwhelming miasma that had escaped. He stepped inside and stared at the body crumpled up on the dirt floor.

"Stop, Linds. Don't go any further. We need to call nine-one-one, again."

Jed was blocking the doorway, so I had to lean over and around him to see the problem.

"Who is that?" I asked.

"I don't have a clue, but I bet Ryan knows who it is," Jed answered as he snapped a photo on his cell phone and dialed 9-1-1.

Chapter 25

Detective Wilson was the legal authority who showed up to answer Jed's call.

"This is getting to be a habit with you people," he said as he frowned at the body sprawled out on the floor. "Did you break the tape and cross the police line?"

"No sir, the tape was already broken. We wanted to check to see if we could find anything that might have been missed in the first search," Jed answered, trying to remain calm after the snide remark from the detective.

"Do you know who that is, lying on the floor dead?" asked Detective Wilson.

"No sir," answered Jed as I shook my head in agreement.

"Would your son know who this is?" probed Detective Wilson.

"Maybe, but he is still in a coma," I said sadly.

"Do the doctors have any idea about if or when he will awaken from the coma?" asked the detective as politely as he could manage.

"They said he is showing signs of coming out of it, but I can't tell there is a difference. Have you found out any more information about my daughters?" I asked.

"Yes, we have a couple of leads that we are checking on," the detective answered.

"Can you tell me about them?" I pleaded.

"No, Ms. Harris. They're only leads. I don't want the two of you butting in where you shouldn't," he said sternly.

I clamped my mouth shut so I wouldn't give him a piece of my mind. It was really hard for me not to rip him a new one.

"Jed, we need to leave so these gentlemen can take care of business," I said as I cast a glance to the outside through the window that was still in one piece.

We walked to the door so I could point off to the right to indicate which way I wanted to walk. Of course, it was not toward the vehicle, but Jed followed me anyway.

"Where are we going?" he asked.

"I saw someone over there who was not a cop. I wanted to see if she is still there," I answered.

"She?" he asked.

"Over there," I said as I pointed to an area in front of me.

"Yeah, okay. Now what?" he asked.

"I want to talk with her," I said.

We both took off running toward the girl, who was hiding in the bushes. Jed ran to the right and I went to the left so we could catch up with her and somewhat block her escape.

"Miss, young lady, don't be afraid. We are not the police," I said in a moderate tone. I didn't want the legal authorities in and around the clubhouse to hear me.

The girl stopped and looked at me.

"What do you want?" she hissed.

"Do you live around here?" I asked.

"What if I do?"

"Well, I was trying to find out who had been using that cabin. It's the one where the police are searching," I explained.

"I've seen them come and go, but I don't really know them,"

66

the girl answered.

"Did you see them take two young girls inside the cabin against their will?" I asked.

"Yeah, I did, and they didn't look too happy."

"How long ago did you see them?" I asked excitedly.

"What's it to you, lady?"

"Those girls are my daughters, and we are trying to find them," I answered, praying she would give me more information.

"You're their mother?"

"Yes. Do you know where they went?" I asked.

"I heard one of them say they were going farther up the mountain. I don't know where, but that's what I heard," she said in a whisper.

"Do you know who the young man inside the clubhouse is? He's dead, you know."

"I don't know him, but he's one of them who brought the girls to the clubhouse," she explained.

"What's your name?" I asked.

"I'm not going to tell you. I don't want to get involved. I don't want those guys hunting me down," said the girl, and she took off running.

Chapter 26

"Jed, we need to take a drive further on up the mountain. Maybe we can find the new clubhouse," I suggested.

"Do you want them to shoot at us again?" he asked skeptically.

"No, I want to find my daughters," I snapped. I didn't mean to snap at him, but I just couldn't help it.

"Okay, okay, let's go."

"I'm sorry I snapped. I'm so worried," I said in sincere apology.

We drove slowly up the mountain and pulled over at the sightseeing observation spots so those behind us would think we were there for the scenic beauty.

We were searching for anyone who might belong to the drug club.

"Not much traffic today, is there?" I asked.

"I guess it's about normal. The sightseers are the reason they keep this road paved," said Jed.

"What about the people who live on this mountain?" I asked.

"Those are few and far between. I'm sure you have noticed that," he replied.

"What I have noticed are little, unpaved roads spiraling off the paved road," I said.

"Yes, and one of those should take us to where the new club-house is located. Are you ready to try one of them?" he asked.

"Which one?"

"That one right there," he said pointing to his left. "It looks like it has been traveled on recently."

"Should we park along the paved road and then walk?" I asked nervously.

"That's a good idea. We need to stay behind the brush and trees, where we can hopefully avoid any flying bullets."

We walked to the rutted road and moved off to the side, where we leaned over and squatted down to try to hide from sight. Of course, we didn't know from which direction the sight line was. We also didn't know how far up the road we needed to travel before we found what we were looking for, in the form of a cabin of some kind.

It was hard traveling, but we finally reached the end of the rutted road.

"Now which way?" I asked Jed.

"The grass is mashed down over there. We need to follow that path," he said as he led the way.

"Down! Get down," he whispered.

Automatically I squatted and looked around to see what the problem might be.

"What?" I asked, when I couldn't spot a reason.

"Up ahead, I saw movement. It was just a flash of color," he explained. "I hope whoever it was didn't see us."

I didn't know whether I should move forward or stay put right where I was.

"Let's see if we can move forward a little bit," said Jed.

"Do you think we should go back to the car?" I asked.

"Yes, I do...but if we want to find the girls, we need to keep moving," he answered honestly.

I was scared, but I was also worried. We needed to find

Ellen and Emily, and hope that nothing horrible had happened to them.

"Get down," Jed whispered harshly.

I tried to flatten myself as close to the ground as I could get without actually lying down. When I raised my head to focus on what was ahead of me, I saw the gun.

Chapter 27

"Get up!" said the voice behind the gun,
I did just that. I stood up and looked him in the eye.

"Get that gun out of my face," I snarled. I'd had enough of this sneaking around and dodging guns and bullets.

My direct statement must have struck the wielder of the gun as funny because he started laughing. Nonetheless, he did not move the gun from my face. Actually, he moved it in a little bit closer.

"Who are you?" I demanded. I wasn't going to back down and show him the fear I was feeling.

He didn't answer me.

"What do you want?" I asked loudly.

He motioned with his gun for me to move.

I did move because I wanted to find Jed. I didn't see him anywhere but I didn't call out his name. Maybe this gun toting fellow hadn't seen him. At least, that was what I hoped. He might be able to help me out of this mess.

I must have been walking too slowly because I felt the barrel of the gun poking into my back. I really wanted to tell him where he could put that gun.

"Stop poking me," I whispered.

"Keep moving," he snarled.

"How much further?" I asked.

"Just keep walking," he snapped.

Again with the poking, so I kept walking, getting angrier with each step.

I held my head high so I could see what was ahead of me as I walked, which was a good thing because I saw a sudden flash of color. The color was important because it looked like the shirt Jed was wearing.

I stumbled and fell to the ground. I had scraped my knee, apparently, because it was bleeding through my jeans.

"Get up, lady," hissed the man with the gun.

"I'm trying," I said with a whimper while I pulled the cloth of the jeans away from the bleeding cut.

"Now, lady! Get up and start walking," he snarled and waved the gun at me sticking it directly in front of my face.

While I was on the ground, I scanned the area in front me.

"Jed, where are you?" I whispered softly so my kidnapper couldn't hear me.

"What did you say?" he asked.

"I was asking God for some help," I replied. I hoped God would forgive me for the outright lie.

"I don't think He is going to swoop down here and help you. Just get up and get a move on," he said with a devilish grimace.

"You never know," I said in a smart-alecky tone.

Chapter 28

From my position still sprawled out on the ground, I saw a wonderful sight taking shape.

"Why are you doing this?" I shouted at the gun carrier. I wanted to keep him busy talking to me, not becoming aware of what was happening behind him.

"Get up!" he shouted angrily.

I started to roll over so I could push myself up in a very unladylike fashion. The movement also got me out of the way so Jed could do his thing.

There was a crash and a grunt as the kidnapper fell to the ground. His forward fall barely missed me as I scrambled over to the side and out of the way.

"What did you hit him with?" I asked in amazement.

"A rock. That's all I could find. Hopefully, I didn't kill him, but I was afraid of what he was going to do to you," explained Jed excitedly.

"I was afraid of that very same thing," I said in agreement.

Jed helped me get up off the ground and held on to me while I put pressure on my damaged leg, the knee to be specific.

"Can you walk?" he asked with concern.

"I have to in order to get out of here," I replied.

"If you can't, you can wait here while I go get help," he said sympathetically.

"No, not on your life," I said. I hobbled a step or two to show him I could walk.

"Are you sure?" he asked.

"Yes, but what are we going to do with that pile of flesh lying on the ground?" I asked.

"I'm going to grab his gun, rouse him up, and make him lead us to the rest of the club members," he said. Jed grabbed the gun that had been laying on the ground where it had fallen out of the kidnapper's hand.

We heard a moan coming from the mound of flesh. His only movement was to reach toward his bleeding head. He pulled his hand away to see the blood that was on it.

"What the..." he sputtered when he saw the blood.

He forced himself up to a sitting position and looked around, patting the ground and feeling for the gun.

"You looking for this?" asked Jed with a big smile. He hoisted the gun up so it could be seen.

The man who had been threatening me was now the one being threatened. That made me feel a little better, at least for the moment.

"What are you going to do?" the kidnapper growled.

"What were you going to do to me?" I snapped.

"Nothing" the kidnapper said solemnly.

"If nothing, why were you holding a gun on me?" I asked angrily.

"Um...I...uh..." he stammered.

"Get up and get moving," commanded Jed.

"Where to?" asked the kidnapper.

"To wherever you were taking me," I snapped. "We want to meet all of your friends."

"You don't want to do that," he snarled. "You're strangers;

74

they will kill you, along with me for bringing you to the club-house."

"That's a chance we will have to take," said Jed, motioning forward with the gun to get everyone moving in one direction.

Chapter 29

We were moving slowly as we followed a poorly defined path that could barely be discerned through the undergrowth.

I pulled my cell phone from my pocket and discovered the phrase *no service*. I sighed as I shoved it back into my pocket.

My knee had finally stopped oozing blood, but the pain was growing with each step.

The kidnapper was watching his surroundings closely. I was sure he wanted to make a run for it, but wasn't willing to challenge Jed at that time.

He stopped walking, so we all had to stop.

"Move," said Jed harshly.

"No," said the kidnapper.

"I said move it," Jed snapped.

"If we go any further, someone will take a shot at us," the kidnapper answered solemnly.

"Then you need to stay up front so they can see it's you. We will be right behind you," said Jed. "If we stand directly behind you, then they won't see us, I hope."

"If they do, we are all dead," warned the kidnapper.

We kept walking with our heads on a swivel. We were aware of our own noise and listened intently for sounds that we didn't make.

I saw what looked like a roughly structured building through the trees off to my right.

"It's over here," I said as I pointed to my right. "He needs to be in front so move over here."

Jed nudged the kidnapper with the gun, "Move it."

The kidnapper moved to his right, Jed followed directly behind him, and I brought up the rear.

A shout came from the clubhouse.

"Mountain, is that you?" asked a single voice.

"Yes, it's me."

He kept walking and we stayed close, directly behind him. When we arrived at the door, the kidnapper ducked and the man inside cocked his weapon, preparing to shoot.

I dived one way and Jed dived the opposite direction, so the bullet traveled between us without causing any bloodletting.

Jed raised his gun and fired at the man who shot at us, then whirled around and aimed at the kidnapper, Mountain.

The man Jed shot was holding onto the fleshy part of his upper arm. Blood was trickling through his fingers.

Mountain was rubbing at his injured head and moaning.

"Both of you guys listen up!" shouted Jed. "We are looking for the two girls you and your buddies took from the house. Where can we find them?"

Mumbles and shrugs emanated from both of them.

"Shoot them, Jed! If they aren't going to help us, then kill them," I said angrily. Of course, I didn't mean what I was saying about the killing part.

Jed made a show of taking aim.

"Whoa, don't shoot!" said the man with the bleeding arm. "They're in the back, tied up in the outhouse."

"Linds, go check outside while I keep an eye on these two."

Chapter 30

I walked around the clubhouse to the back and spotted the outhouse.

"Emily! Ellen!" I shouted. I prayed I would hear an answer.

I heard muffled sounds—no words, but I could tell there were people inside that outhouse.

I pulled the door open and saw Ellen sitting against the opposite wall with Emily sitting on the area near the open hole. Both girls were wriggling with excitement.

"I'll get you out of here," I whispered as I started pulling at the duct tape wrapped around their hands and feet. I jerked off the pieces of duct tape that covered their mouths. They both screamed from pain but smiled from ear to ear.

When they were both released, I was covered with hugs and kisses that I happily returned to my precious daughters.

"Mom, how did you find us?" asked Emily.

"Persistence and determination," I answered with a glorious smile.

"No, really, Mom, how did you do it?" asked Ellen.

"Well... I was held hostage—by the same guy who grabbed you, I think. Anyway, with Jed's help, I managed to get away from him. Then Jed and I forced him to tell us where you were,"

I said with a sigh.

"What took you so long?" asked Ellen. A huge smile crossed her lips.

At that question, the dam that was holding back the tears broke and I started sobbing.

When Emily and Ellen saw my tears, their eyes filled to brimming over, too; and we all just held onto each other. We had a good cry for happiness.

Once the crying session was over, I ushered the girls out so we could let Jed know that it was time to call the police,

I opened the door to the clubhouse slowly and shouted Jed's name so he would know it was me. Hopefully, taking that precaution would prevent the firing of the gun in his possession.

"Is that you, Linds?" said Jed loudly.

"Yes, Emily and Ellen are with me," I answered as the door opened.

I saw my kidnapper sitting in the corner of the room trussed up like a Thanksgiving turkey.

"You didn't call the police, did you?" I asked Jed.

"Not yet. I was waiting for you to come back in so we could tell them they don't have to look for the girls because we found them ourselves," answered Jed.

I pulled out my cell phone and dialed 9-1-1. I asked for Detective Wilson, who was working on the case for the two missing girls.

"Detective Wilson, may I be of service?" he politely responded to the ringing phone.

"Yes sir, this is Lindsay Harris. We—Jed and I—have found my daughters. We are holding their kidnapper in the clubhouse farther up Route Sixteen, about halfway up the mountain. He is tied up and ready to be hauled off to jail. Just to let you know, he also kidnapped me and held a gun on me until my friend, Jed Thompson, jumped him and took the gun away from him. Will you send someone to pick him up?" I said in a flurry of words. I really wanted him to know that we did all of the work for him.

"Ms. Harris, you stay right where you are. I will be there as soon as possible. Can you give me a more accurate address?" asked the flustered detective.

I gave him the general directions that the clubhouse was located off Route 16, up the first mountain on the Stillwell County side, on a gravel road to the right. That was as explicit as I was able to get.

Chapter 31

Detective Wilson arrived in an unmarked police vehicle, followed by two cruisers with flashing lights and sirens.

I thought it was a little bit too much of a performance, but I didn't say anything to put down the noisy entrance.

Jed stayed with his trussed-up turkey of a kidnapper while I went out to greet the police officers, with my daughters in tow.

"Detective Wilson, I would like you to meet my daughters, Emily and Ellen," I said. I struggled to keep the sarcasm out of my voice.

Detective Wilson walked away from us and headed toward the clubhouse door where Jed was waiting.

"Mr. Thompson, can you tell me what happened here? Why do you have this man tied up?"

I was standing just outside of the door and I thought I knew what the detective was trying to do. In my opinion, he was trying to determine if my side of the story was the same as Jed's version.

When Detective Wilson was satisfied with Jed's response, he asked the officers with him to release the trussed-up kidnapper and handcuff him. He then asked the four of us—Jed, Ellen, Emily, and me—to meet him at the police station to make our statements.

Before making the trip to the police station, I wanted to make a stop at the hospital to check in on Ryan. I had not received a call from the hospital to tell me there was any change in his condition, but I wanted to see for myself.

When I approached ICU, I was again stopped by a police officer. After proving to him I was Ryan's mother, I entered the room.

Ryan was moving around a bit under his restraints, which were keeping him from harming himself. He seemed to be mumbling incoherently.

"Run, Devon, run!" he suddenly shouted.

I reached for his arm to try to calm him, but he continued yelling, "Run, Devon, run!"

Tears overflowed my eyes as I watched my son struggle to rise up from the deep, dark hole his head injury had dug for him.

I had turned to leave when the nurse appeared.

"He is trying very hard to become conscious," she whispered. "I will call you when he is lucid."

"Yes ma'am, please do. I have to go to the police station right now to give them a statement about the events of the day. Please call," I said as I wiped the tears from my eyes.

Everyone was waiting for me in the car, so I hurried out to meet them. We would continue on to the police station.

I walked out the front door and started searching for the SUV containing Jed, Emily and Ellen. I knew where they had initially parked, but the car was not there. I scanned the lot over and over again searching for them.

I walked back to the hospital entrance and stood there like a statue. Hopefully, my group would come back from wherever they went to pick me up.

Finally, I saw the car coming through the parking lot, much faster than it should have been traveling.

"Get in, Linds!" shouted Jed when the car screeched to a halt.

"What's going on?" I asked, slamming the car door. He pressed hard on the gas pedal to move us out of there.

"Ryan's 'friend' tried to block us in. I was afraid of what they were going to do, so I took off and headed toward the police station. That must have discouraged their pursuit of us. Anyway, we need to leave so they won't come back and find us."

We made it to the police station without another incident, where we met with Detective Wilson.

"How do we get that group of hoodlums to leave us alone?" I asked Detective Wilson.

"We are working on this, Ms. Harris," said the detective in a calming tone.

"They were trying to catch me by blocking me in at the hospital parking lot. We got away, but they might do us harm the next time," said Jed. "We can't go outside without taking our lives in our hands."

"Mr. Thompson, can you tell me what kind of car they were driving?" asked Detective Wilson.

"There was more than one car trying to block me in, but I can tell you what they were. I can also give you some of the plate numbers. I only got a couple of them, but that might help," said Jed.

After the four of us made our statements, it was the middle of the night and we were all exhausted.

"Should we go to my house?" I asked Jed.

"Yes, we can take turns keeping watch. We do need to get some rest," he answered.

Chapter 32

J ed took the first watch, which meant that I would go to sleep for four hours or less. As soon as my head hit my pillow, I was out like a light.

The restful sleep didn't last long, maybe an hour, before I heard a crash followed by the loud tinkle of breaking glass.

I rose from my pillow, startled, as I looked around me to see if anyone was in my bedroom. I reached for the lamp so I could make sure no one was hiding from me.

I climbed from my bed, grabbed my robe, and raced to check on the girls and Jed, who was on guard.

Emily and Ellen were still asleep, but Jed was moving around the living room in the dark.

"Jed?" I whispered. "Are you all right?"

I heard another crash and a loud grunt, and it was all happening in the dark. No light had been switched on to illuminate the room, and I didn't know whether or not I should reach for the light switch.

"Jed, where are you?" I whispered.

I heard a sudden intake of breath then he answered, "Over here."

"Should I turn on the light?" I asked.

"If you want to see the mess and the idiot on the floor, go ahead and turn it on," he answered as he struggled to gain control of his breathing.

That statement brought me out of my fear and pushed me toward anger. I flicked the switch and sucked in a breath, because I was looking at total destruction and a bloody body.

"What happened to him?" I asked Jed as I checked to see if the body was breathing.

"First, he broke the window; second, he started crawling in through the hole; and third, I picked up your side chair and whomped him on the head with it," he explained.

"Is he alive?" I asked, as I stared at the bloody body of a young man.

"He's still breathing, as far as I can tell. I've called nine-one-one and asked for Detective Wilson. Hopefully, he and his bunch can put a stop to this, but only time will tell. Maybe we are getting to the end of the people who are trying to hurt us. I really want to find out if Ryan's friend Devon is all right, especially after you told me that Ryan was calling his name," said Jed.

A police cruiser pulled into my driveway with sirens blaring and lights flashing. The officer exited his vehicle with gun drawn, pointing it at me as I stood on the front porch. I was getting tired of being on the wrong end of the weapon, but what could I do about it? The officer was only being cautious.

"Officer, the trouble is inside," I shouted.

"Raise your hands—now!" he shouted back at me.

"Sure," I said as I fought to hold my thoughts to myself. "I'm one of the victims, not the criminal. He is inside and unconscious, hopefully."

He motioned for me to step aside but I continued to keep my hands raised. He made a quick search of me before he proceeded to go inside the house, again, with his gun in hand.

I followed him and I walked toward Jed who was keeping an

eye on the unconscious man on the floor.

"Tell me what happened here," said the police officer as he waved his gun at Jed.

"You see that broken window right there? And that rock over there next to the wall?" said an exasperated Jed as he pointed to the rock.

"Yes," responded the officer.

"That man lying there on the floor broke the window and crawled through the hole; then I hit him over the head with that broken chair. Of course, it wasn't broken before I hit him."

"Who is he?" asked the officer.

"I believe he is part of the gang who has been harassing us. They actually put her son in the hospital, and he is still there. As far as that man is concerned, I don't know his name so you will have to check his pockets," said Jed.

"Why was he after you?" asked the officer.

"It's a long story, and it's related to drugs," I answered. "You should talk with Detective Wilson; he can fill you in on everything. But in the meantime, you should arrest this guy and charge him with breaking and entering, if for nothing else."

Chapter 33

The arrest of our latest attacker finally happened, and we were allowed to try to clean up after the crime scene investigators finished what they had to do.

"I'm going to have to go buy some plywood to board up the window. You certainly don't want any more uninvited visitors," said Jed as we surveyed the mess.

"I think there's some you can use in the storage building out back. I'll find the hammer and nails so you can get started," I said, my voice tinged with tears.

"Don't fall apart, Linds. We can get through this," he said. He hugged me close for comfort.

"I hope he's the last one to come after us," I mumbled into the hug.

We had been instructed to go to the sheriff's office, once again, to give a statement.

"We need to speak with Detective Wilson," I said to the officer at the front desk. I stood there for a few minutes until Detective Wilson appeared. By that time, Jed had parked the car and stood beside me.

"What happened this time?" the detective asked me.

"Not much, except that someone else tried to kill us," I said, sarcasm evident in my response. "We were told to come in here to make a statement about the latest incident."

"Let's get started," said Detective Wilson, as he displayed what appeared to be concern.

We were led to one of the interrogation rooms, again.

"Before we get started with the latest attempt on our lives, we need to ask if you found Ryan's friend, Devon," said Jed.

"I'm sorry to have to tell you, but I believe he was the young man found on Route Sixteen at the side of the road. I believe it was around the same time you were there," said Detective Wilson. "Did you not see him when you were there locating your daughter?"

"No sir, we did not. How did he die?" I asked.

"He was shot in the back of the head, execution style."

"He was just a little boy," I said, tears rolling down my cheeks.

"This has got to stop," said Jed. He tried to console me again with an arm around my shoulders.

"Ms. Harris, I am posting a car on your street to catch any new attempts. It will be unmarked for your safety," said Detective Wilson.

"I wish you had done that before my window was broken. Thank you for doing it now," I said sincerely. "Do you still have an officer posted outside my son's hospital room?"

"Yes ma'am, but there have been no more threats since the bomb scare."

"Are you going to keep a person posted there?" I asked.

"No, after today we will not have anyone posted because of the inactivity."

"Do you have all of the gang under lock and key?" I demanded.

"We have several of them, but we don't know how many are involved. So... No, we don't have them all. We are looking for the person or persons who killed the young boy we found. He appears to have been one of the gang."

"He was killed because he was a friend of my son. So that only leaves my son, Ryan, as the remaining lose end. You need to keep him protected," I demanded angrily.

"I'll see what I can do," said the apologetic detective.

"I'm going to go see if my son has improved. Hopefully, he has come out of his coma," I said as I turned to leave.

"I haven't received a call from the hospital notifying me that he is able to talk," said the detective. "Please let me know if he is improving."

I walked away, totally frustrated.

Chapter 34

We drove home to pick up the girls so we could all go to the hospital to check on Ryan. I didn't want to leave Emily and Ellen unattended for long periods of time for fear that something bad would happen to them again.

The ride to the hospital was quiet. I think we were all waiting for the next shoe to drop, causing us to face another disaster.

We walked to the front entrance and were stopped at the door by a big, burly guy identifying himself as a police officer. He was dressed in jeans and a sport shirt, so I asked for some kind of identification.

That was the wrong thing to do.

He immediately whipped out a handgun and pointed it toward all four of us.

I pulled one of the girls behind me and Jed did the same. I didn't want him to have four targets; the two of us were more than enough.

"What's the problem, officer?" I asked. I tried to keep his farce going to prevent his need to shoot at us.

I looked around and we were surrounded by a group of scruffy looking young men with their hands behind their backs, as if they were hiding something. My thought was that each of them was hiding some kind of weapon.

"What is it you want?" asked Jed angrily.

"All of you, along with your son," said the original, big, bad, and ugly man we had met upon trying to enter the hospital.

"Why?" I sputtered.

"We need to tie up some lose ends and eliminate a few problems," he answered in a surly tone.

They all started to step in towards us. They were getting too close for comfort.

"Back off!" I yelled fiercely.

There was a sudden flurry of activity.

"Get down!" shouted Jed as he dived for cover. We all followed his command and kissed the floor in the lobby of the hospital.

Bullets started flying over our heads, but thank God, they weren't coming at the four of us.

I saw the big guy fall in front of me, followed by the thuds of several more bodies crashing to the floor.

When it was quiet, I tried to stand up, but one of those bodies had fallen across my legs. I felt my cell phone vibrate in my pocket, so I tried to dig it out while trying to release my legs from underneath the body.

"Hello," I whispered breathlessly into the phone.

"Ms. Harris, this is Stillwell ICU. Your son, Ryan, is out of his coma," said an efficient-sounding voice.

"Thank you, I will be there as soon as possible," I responded with a smile crossing my lips. At least, something good was happening this long and terrible day.

A couple of police officers hoisted the body off of me, cuffing him as he struggled to come to. They also helped Emily and Ellen up from the floor. Jed was a little slower getting up, and I was afraid he had been hit by a flying bullet.

He brushed himself off and checked out the blood spots that were on his clothing.

"None of that blood is mine," he whispered to me.

"Ryan's awake," I told him. "Let's all go up and see him."

We all boarded the elevator to go to ICU, where we were met by Detective Wilson.

"Ms. Harris, I think we have all of them now. And we know that the big guy who was preventing you from entering the hospital was the one who killed young Devon," he said with a smile.

We went into see Ryan, two at a time. I was first in, but also last out. I needed to know why he had gotten himself involved in a drug gang.

"I was doing what you do, mom. I was snooping. I really didn't want to be a part of it, but I couldn't get out of it."

At that point, my only response was that *Snooping Can Be Regrettable*.

ABOUT THE AUTHOR

Linda Hudson Hoagland of Tazewell, Virginia, a graduate of Southwest Virginia Community College, has won acclaim for many of her novels that include *Snooping Can Be Dangerous, Snooping Can Be Contagious, Snooping Can Be Devious, Snooping Can Be Doggone Deadly, Snooping Can Be Helpful–Sometimes, Snooping Can Be Uncomfortable, Snooping Can Be Scary, The Best Darn Secret, Onward & Upward,* and *Missing Sammy,* all published by Jan-Carol Publishing Inc.

Hoagland has written other fiction, nonfiction, poetry, and short stories that have been included in many anthologies, including *Broken Petals, Easter Lilies, These Haunted Hills, Wild Daisies,* and *Snowy Trails.*

Hoagland is a retired Tazewell County Schools System employee, where she worked as a purchase order clerk for almost 23 years. She is a proud mother of two sons.

COMING SOON

Lindsay Harris discovers that a Merry Christmas is not in her future when she uncovers a murder that seems to pull her into the classification of being a murder suspect as an unhappy neighbor. Her children have the task of proving her innocence. The Harris family proves that SNOOPING CAN BE UN-MERRY.

LINDSAY HARRIS
MURDER MYSTERY SERIES

BY LINDA HUDSON HOAGLAND

JAN-CAROL PUBLISHING, INC.

Linda Hudson Hoagland has authored and published many books, including poetry, and is an accomplished writer. She has received recognition and numerous awards throughout her writing career.

WWW.LINDASBOOKSANDANGELS.COM